Distributed in the United States by North-South Books Inc., New York.

First published in the United States, Great Britain, Canada,
Australia and New Zealand in 1992 by North-South Books,
an imprint of Nord-Süd Verlag AG, Gossau Zürich, Switzerland.

Library of Congress Cataloging-in-Publication Data
Watts, Bernadette.
[Sonne und Wind. English]
The wind and the sun: an Aesop fable / retold and
illustrated by Bernadette Watts.
Translation of: Sonne und Wind.
Summary: The sun and the wind test their strength by seeing
which of them can force a man to remove his cloak.
ISBN 1-55858-162-6 (trade binding)
ISBN 1-55858-163-4 (library binding)
[1. Fables.] I. Aesop. II. Title.
PZ8.2.W35Wi 1992
398.26 dc20 [E] 92-2653

British Library Cataloguing in Publication Data
Aesop
The Wind and the Sun: Fable from Aesop
I. Title II. Watts, Bernadette
823.914
ISBN 1-55855-162-6

1 3 5 7 9 10 8 6 4 2

Printed in Belgium

The Wind and the Sun

An Aesop Fable ❖ Retold and Illustrated by

Bernadette Watts

North-South Books

NEW YORK

One day, the Wind and the Sun had a
quarrel. Each boasted that he was the stronger.

As they argued, they looked down and saw a
man walking along the road, going from one
town to another. His cloak was fluttering
around his shoulders.

"I propose a test," said the Wind. "Whichever one of us can tear the cloak from the back of that man is the stronger. Do you agree?"

"Of course," said the Sun, smiling warmly.

The Wind took the first turn. He blew so hard that the trees began to sway back and forth. Kite strings were torn from children's fingers. Clothes hung out to dry were blown off the line.

The man shivered and held tightly to his cloak.

Then the Wind blew up a gale. Leaves and branches were torn from trees. Everyone hurried indoors for shelter.

The man leaned into the wind and held his cloak even tighter. Every time it blew about, he gathered it back around himself. The mighty Wind blew and blew, but he could not tear the cloak away.

"You have failed," said the Sun. "And now it is my turn."

When the Wind stopped the flowers turned
their faces to the Sun and the birds began to
sing. The children came outside again to play.
It was very warm.

The man felt hot and thirsty. He came to an inn and stopped to drink a cup of water.

The Sun shone brighter and the man became hotter and hotter. He pulled off his boots. It was much too hot to wear them.

At last he came to a stream. He sat on the bank and dipped his feet in the cool water. But the Sun still shone warmly on his back.

The man could bear the heat of the day no longer. He decided to lie down in the shade of a tree to rest. He took off his cloak and laid it across the grass.

"I have won," said the Sun to the Wind. "As you can see, it is easier to influence people with gentleness than with force."

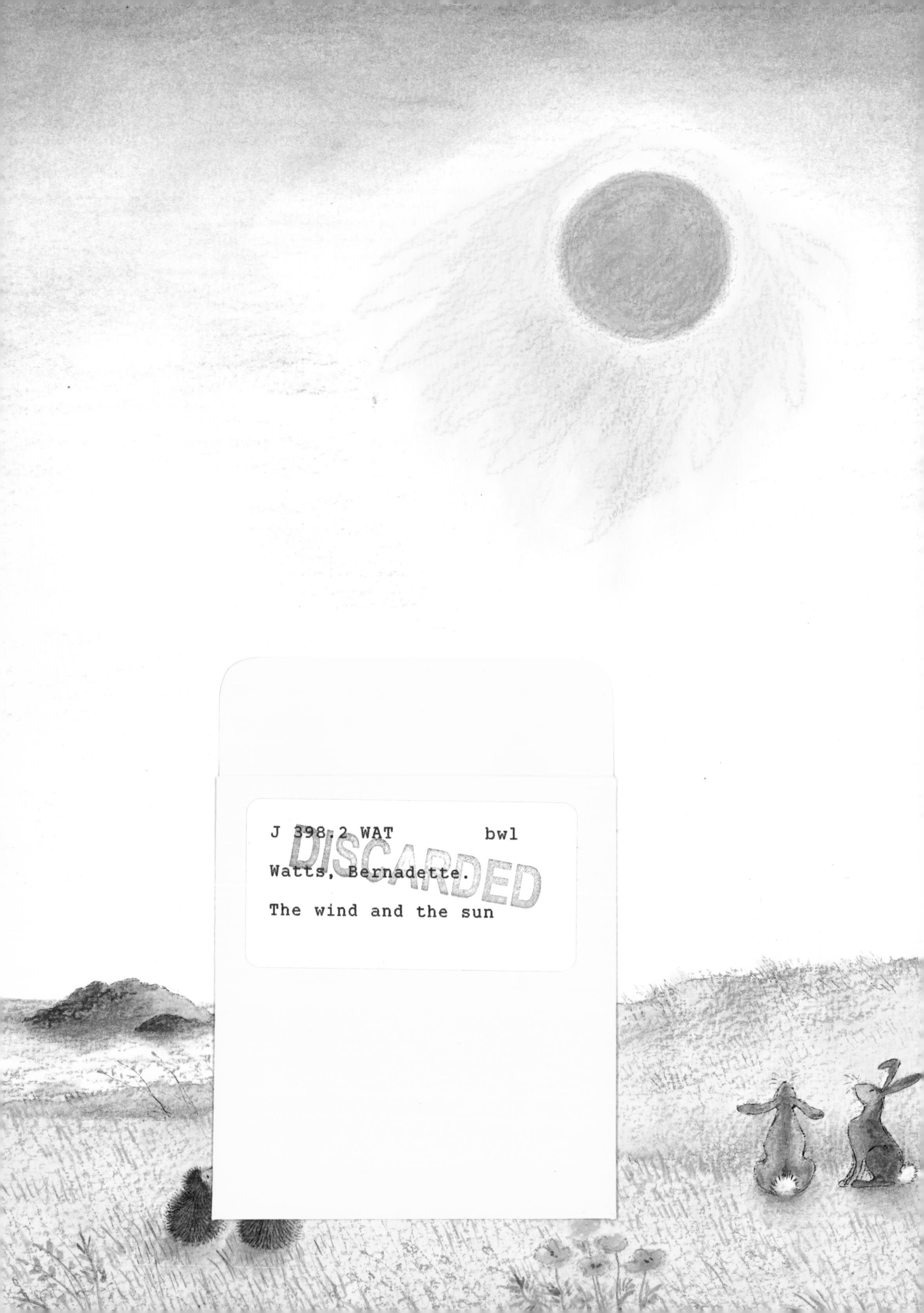